# Fairy Berries

ALLISON LEIGH STEVENS

© 2020 Allison Leigh Stevens
*Fairy Berries*

First edition, December 2020

JustOneYou Books
Grand Rapids, MI
allisonleighstevens.com

Artwork: Cheryl Crouthamel
Publishing and Design Services: MelindaMartin.me

*Fairy Berries* is under copyright protection. No part of this book may be used or reproduced in any manner whatsoever without written permission except in the case of brief quotations embodied in critical articles and reviews. Printed in the United States of America. All rights reserved.

This is a work of fiction and a product of the author's imagination.

ISBN: 978-1-7351958-2-7 (paperback)

Dedicated to Lillian Grace.
You are my inspiration.

CHAPTER ONE

# The Enchanted Forest

Many years ago, in a place far away, there was a forest. Some say it was enchanted. Trees stretched far into the sky and gave the animals plenty of space to run and play hide-and-seek. Flowers sprinkled the forest floor. The wings of butterflies glowed when in flight, leaving a rainbow of colors behind them in the sky.

But what made this forest especially charming were the tiny glittery-winged fairies! They were rarely seen. On very quiet days, if you closed your eyes and quieted your mind, you could hear their laughter and chatter like tinkling bells.

The fairy sisters—Lilly, Faye, Jada, and Felicia—lived in the fairy village, hidden deep

## Fairy Berries

in the forest. They had a very important job: caring for the fairy berries. The fairies rose with the sun and hovered over the berry patch to spot unwanted weeds and yank them out. Every so often after they had watered the vines, they would sprinkle fairy dust on the berries to make them a bit plumper and juicier. The fairies twirled and laughed and sang as they picked the berries. They knew eating a fairy berry could make even the grouchiest animal feel happiness and joy.

Now what would an enchanted forest be without an evil witch? She too lived in the forest, plotting ways to rule over all the animals. It's no surprise to you, I'm sure, that she didn't like the fairies one bit. Steam poured from the witch's ears when she thought about the smiling fairies.

Scratching her purple hair, Lilly asked, "Why wouldn't the witch want to have a happy heart and be nice? Does she prefer to have a heart as cold as ice?" Her sisters giggled because she made a rhyme, but Lilly was seriously confused by the witch's choices and flew away shaking her head and mumbling, "I just don't get it."

# Fairy Berries

Faye simply said, "She's a witch, Lilly. She's doing what a witch does."

The witch dreamed of someday ruling over the forest from her stone castle and controlling all the animals in the woods. The witch became jealous of the fairies and the power they had. She came up with a plan to get rid of the fairies and their berries.

CHAPTER TWO

# Wally

"Mom!" Wally shouted from his bedroom. "Can I go outside and play?" Wally was a weasel who spent as much time as he could playing outside with his friends. He lived in the enchanted forest with his mom and dad in a cozy house at the bottom of a tall oak tree near Glitter Creek.

"You may go for a little bit, Wally, but don't be gone long. Dinner will be ready in thirty minutes." Fresh bread baking in the oven made Wally's mouth water.

"Ok, thanks. I'll be back in time for supper." He ran out the door, straight into his father who was

# Fairy Berries

planting flowers along the front of the house. His father said, "Hey, there, not so fast! Where are you off to in such a hurry?"

"I'm going to play with my friends until dinner is ready," Wally said, secretly hoping to see a fairy.

"Ok, buddy, have fun." His father reached out and patted Wally on the back.

When Wally reached the clearing in the middle of the woods, Andy the racoon waved him down. "Hi, Wally! We're playing hide and seek. Want to join us?"

Alice the squirrel was there, and she jumped up and down, clapping her hands. Taylor the rabbit ran up to Wally and they did their special handshake. They jumped high in the air, slapped hands, shook their behinds, and said, "Walla-Tay, Walla-Tay, Walla, Walla, Walla-Tay."

# Fairy Berries

Alice squealed and rolled on the ground laughing at Wally and Taylor. Andy just shook his head and said, "You guys are nuts," which made Alice laugh even harder.

After Alice pulled herself together, she stood up, shook her tail, and wiped the dirt off her fur. "Ok, I'll count to ten and you three go hide. One, two, three," Alice slowly recited.

Wally's eyes darted across the field and spotted a tree. He crawled through the tall grasses to hide behind it, but as he got closer, he saw a hole in the middle of the tree trunk. He wiggled his way in and waited. *No one will find me here!* thought Wally.

# Fairy Berries

Alice called out, "Wally! Taylor! Andy! Ready or not, here I come!" Wally waited, but Alice sounded far away looking for Taylor and Andy. He played with a piece of bark, and after several minutes, he rested his head on a pillow of soft green moss; his eyes got heavy and he dozed off.

Wally woke with a start. *How long have I been in here?* He listened; he didn't hear anything, not even the birds, and he didn't hear his friends, either. It was as quiet as an early snowy morning.

He pulled his arms and legs out of the tree hole and brushed off his pants. He looked for his friends, but they were nowhere to be seen. *Oh, no! I was supposed to be home in time for dinner!*

# Fairy Berries

His heart raced as he broke through shrubs and thistles to get home. He burst through the front door shouting "Mom? Dad?" He stood in the middle of the kitchen, with his eyes wide open. The furniture was overturned and there was a pot of soup left on the stove. He repeated, "Mom? Dad?" No one answered.

Wally explored the entire house, calling out for his parents, opening every door, even the cupboards, to see if his parents were there.

He went outside again and searched the yard. The flowers his dad had planted were brown and drooping over. Wally bent over to touch one and it broke off. *How can this be?*

# Fairy Berries

Wally's eyes flooded with tears when he realized his parents were gone. His head slumped down, and his shoulders shook; he was all alone. He sat down beside the creek, shivering as the cool water trickled over his feet. *Where are my parents? They wouldn't just leave me all by myself. Something bad has happened, and I don't know what to do.*

Just as he was thinking it would be a good idea to go to Taylor's house, the leaves crunched behind him and he froze. His imagination ran wild and he thought, *Is it a bear? Did a bear attack my mom and dad?* He jerked his head toward the sound and scrambled to stand up.

# Fairy Berries

Instead of a bear, he saw a woman with dark hair that traveled in soft curls on her shoulders. Her eyes were the greenest he'd ever seen, like emeralds, and her milky white skin glowed. She  looked so fancy in her long sparkling blue dress. She clutched a cloth bag and said, "Why are you out here alone, little weasel?"

Wally felt dizzy in this woman's presence, and it took a second for him to remember why he was out there. He recovered from the trance he was in and wiped his eyes and said, "My parents are gone, and I think a bear—" he stopped because his throat tightened, and he couldn't finish his sentence.

The woman's eyes darted around the woods as if a bear was lurking behind a tree. She said, "I saw a bear earlier," confirming what he was already thinking.

Wally continued, "I was playing with my friends in the clearing and when I came home, everything was destroyed, and …." He looked at the creek as his eyes filled with tears.

The woman set down the bag she was holding and took a step toward Wally. She asked in the sweetest voice, "Tell me your name. I'm Walinda."

"I'm Wally," he said without looking up.

"Wally, tell me, where did you say you were when your parents, uh, disappeared?"

"I was playing hide and seek in the clearing," he mumbled. "I wanted to see fairies at first, but my friends—"

"Fairies?!" Walinda said, trying to contain the anger in her voice as thoughts of these little creatures started spinning in her head. She thought, *Maybe this weasel will be the one to finally help me find those pesky little—*

Her thoughts were interrupted by Wally's weeping. He shouted, "I never should have gone!" He put his head down and covered his face with his hands.

"Wally, you can come stay with me. I live alone and would welcome the company."

# Fairy Berries

Wally didn't want to leave the house, in case his parents returned. But he didn't want to sleep alone either. His stomach ached because

he hadn't eaten supper. He imagined the delicious smells of his mother's cooking floating through their house and he felt so sad. His head drooped, and he plopped down on the ground and laid there.

"Your choice," Walinda said. "Stay out here. It's up to you." She turned to retrieve her bag, effortlessly throwing it over her shoulder, and stomped away. "But there are scary things in the dark. Things that could eat you!" She yelled over her shoulder as she swayed down the path.

Wally sat up and said, "Wait! I-I-I'll come with you." He scrambled up the creek's bank and ran toward Walinda.

CHAPTER THREE

# Walinda's House

Wally followed the woman deeper into the dark woods. Was it his imagination or was Walinda's hair changing? Little rivers of gray inched down her hair. Wally rubbed his eyes thinking they were playing tricks on him. Finally, Walinda stopped and said, "This is where I live." Wally gasped when he saw the old tattered house in front of him.

The shutters on the house were falling off, and most of the white paint had peeled back, exposing old gray wood. How could Walinda live in a broken-down house like this?

The front door creaked like an old haunted house when Walinda opened it, and one single candle burned on the round wooden table in the kitchen. Curtains of cobwebs hung from the windows, dust balls littered the floor, and crumbs dotted the counters.

As if Walinda could read Wally's thoughts, she plopped the bag on to a chair (*clunk!*) and put her hands up to her chin as if she were praying. "I'm building a new, bigger, taller house—a castle! You will be a great help to me."

The house smelled musty and Wally's nose tickled. He tried to hold back a sneeze and catch the pillow and blanket Walinda tossed in his direction. She said, "You'll sleep in that corner over there."

*Mother and Father used to tuck me in at night in my soft warm bed and read me a story. This isn't like home at all*, Wally thought. As Walinda climbed the stairs to her room, Wally curled up in the corner and cried himself to sleep.

The next morning, Wally jumped at the sounds of Walinda banging pots and pans. He hoped that she was making breakfast because his stomach growled.

He yawned and tip-toed the few steps toward the big black pot in the fireplace and saw that she

# Fairy Berries

wasn't cooking anything that looked like breakfast. Gooey green stuff bubbled in the pot and smelled like dirty socks. Walinda leaned over and chanted,

> "Onions, garlic, cat hair, oil!
> Turn up the heat to watch them boil.
> A castle for me this potion will make—"

# Fairy Berries

Walinda stopped. She saw Wally standing behind her, so she hunched closer to the boiling goop, encircled her arms, and whispered the rest of her chant. The house grew darker and all the air in the room seemed to vanish. Wally felt dizzy. He grabbed the back of the kitchen chair to steady himself, and it slid across the dust. *Is Walinda a-a-a WITCH?!*

# Fairy Berries

Wally's friends had talked about a witch that hid in the forest, but he thought they were only telling stories to scare each other. According to legend, she was angry when her mother died in the forest, and she'd been on a quest for more power and control of the forest ever since.

Walinda whipped her head around and glared at him.

Wally blinked and swallowed and said, "I think I'll be going. I-I want to look for my parents. They're probably still hiding from the bear."

The witch threw her head back and laughed through her wide-open mouth. "You think you can just leave? Silly little creature; you are going to build my castle." Her eyes stared straight at Wally and said, "And then you will find the fairies."

CHAPTER FOUR

# The Bag of Rocks

Wally's heart was beating so fast and hard that he thought for sure Walinda could hear it. How on earth could he build her castle? His eyes were fixed on the witch when she turned, her hair flying like a fan around her head.

"Follow me," Walinda ordered Wally. She marched outside and took him to the edge of her yard. There were no flowers and no butterflies or animals, not even the birds chirped. The pain in his belly wasn't only from hunger. He was afraid of Walinda and he missed his parents.

Walinda ignored the rumbling coming from Wally's stomach and barked at him, "You must pick up all the rocks throughout this field and pile them up over there." She pointed to the top of a hill. "That is where my castle will be." She rubbed

# Fairy Berries

her hands together. With a smirk, she mumbled, "I'll be the most powerful in the forest!"

Wally shuffled over to some rocks and bent over, picking up as many as he could carry. He struggled up the hill and dropped them at the top, just as he was told to do.

After several hours, Walinda showed up to inspect his work. She paced in circles as she spoke, "You would be all alone out in the forest if it weren't for me. This is the least you can do to thank me for taking you in. You'll do this every morning until my castle is complete."

Walinda traipsed back inside the house, leaving Wally wondering if he should take this opportunity to escape into the woods. Before he could finish his thought, she came flying out of the house with the same cloth bag she had placed

on the kitchen chair the night before.

"Now, I want you to go out into the forest and fill this bag with as many rocks as you can."

Wally's heart fell. He thought he was finished with his work. But the witch continued, "Never lose this bag or take any of the rocks out!" She leaned down close to Wally's face, almost nose to nose, and repeated, "Keep this bag with you at all times, never lose it, and never take any rocks out. This bag is the only thing keeping you safe." She stood up straight and held the bag out to Wally.

He hesitated, but then he reached out and took it. He peeked in the bag and noticed that there were two rocks sitting in the bottom. Walinda's eyes glowed green, and her mouth was turned up in a half smile.

"I'm warning you: I will know if you take any rocks out. Now, hurry up, I expect you to serve me dinner at 6:00 p.m. sharp; I'll be hungry as a bear!" Walinda chuckled as she marched back into the house.

The witch didn't have to worry about Wally losing the bag or any of the rocks, because he was

# Fairy Berries

so afraid of what might happen to him if he did.

CHAPTER FIVE

# The Fairies

Wally ventured deep into the woods, putting rocks in the bag, dragging it with him as it got heavier. Occasionally, he'd pick it up to see how long he could carry it.

The farther he walked, the taller the trees reached and the greener the grass grew. The flowers were big and colorful, smelling of sweet honeysuckle. The birds sang and flew in circles around the trees. This place was enchanted. Just as he was about to pick up the bag again, he heard something. Could it be the bear? No, unless bears giggled. He quickly hid in the bushes to see who was talking and laughing.

He peaked through the leaves and a streak of yellowgreenpurplepink whizzed by. Once they were past him, glittery flakes of gold fell softly

# Fairy Berries

to the ground. *Fairies!* He had to stop himself from shouting, "I found fairies!" He smiled as he watched them fly just above the green grasses and flowers. They had sparkly wings and were smaller than a hummingbird. Their hair and dresses matched in colors of yellow, pink, purple and green, and they spoke to one another in kind and playful voices.

## Fairy Berries

"They'll never find us over here," two fairies giggled. Jada had pink hair, and Felicia had yellow hair. They flew behind a big rock. Wally stayed hidden.

Wally's heart beat fast with excitement. He calmed his heart by slowly breathing in and out as he watched to see what the fairies were doing. A few minutes passed, and he heard Faye, the green-haired fairy say, "Hey, Lilly, where did Jada and Felicia go?"

Lilly, the fairy with purple hair, answered, "I don't know. They were here a minute ago. They're probably hiding from us!"

Lilly and Faye laughed and whispered in each other's ears. They flew away and hid behind an oak tree.

Wally kept his hand over his mouth until he heard Jada and Felicia fairies say, "Why aren't our sisters hunting for us? Let's just go find them instead."

Then as fast as they could fly, Jada and Felicia whizzed out from behind the rock and went right toward the big tree where Faye and

# Fairy Berries

Lilly were hiding. When they got close, Faye and Lilly zoomed out from behind the tree and said, "Got ya!"

The two were startled. They tumbled backwards, and fairy dust went everywhere. All four fairies did flips in the air and laughed, which sounded like music dancing through a flute.

The four fairies raced to the top of the tree, their wings vibrating faster than a beetle's. Wally lost sight of the fairies, but then they flew back down the tree and stopped right in front of the bush he was hiding in.

"I won! You three are so slow. What took you so long?" Jada said.

The other sisters looked at Jada with their hands on their hips and all three said at the same time, "Let's do it again."

They raced more and laughed more. Wally's eyes got misty. Their joy reminded him of his friends and how much he missed playing with them.

Faye said, "We'd better get home and work on our berry patch. Soon the berries will be ripe,

# Fairy Berries

and we want to pick them at just the right time.

They began to sing a song.

*A fairy you may meet,*
*A berry you may eat,*
*And when you do,*
*You won't feel blue*
*You'll be so sweet!*

The fairies flew off together singing their song, and Wally wondered what the song meant. His parents had warned him not to eat just any berry in the forest, but it sounded like the fairy berries were special in some way and could make you happy. He wanted to follow the fairies, but it was getting late and he needed to get back to Walinda's house to start dinner.

He looked to make sure no one was around. Arms wrapped around the bag, he tip-toed over to the oak tree and scooped up a handful of fairy dust, stuffed it in his pocket, and heaved the bag toward Walinda's house.

CHAPTER SIX

# Lilly, the Purple Fairy

After making dinner, Wally cleaned the dishes then sat in the corner on his pillow. His arms and shoulders ached from carrying the bag.

Walinda floated up the stairs to her bedroom. Her face glowed from the candle she held in her hands. The further up the stairs she went, the darker his corner became. He lay back and thought about escaping somehow. He stuck his hand in his pocket to feel the fairy dust and dream about how it could help him get back home.

Morning came quickly. Walinda yelled at him to wake up. "Get up! You have a lot of work to do!"

He gathered more rocks around the field near the witch's house and carried them to the top of the hill. After many hours, his heart felt heavy. Wally reached into his pocket. The fairy dust coated his fingers like a glove. If only he could figure out how to use it.

After his chores were complete, Walinda asked, "Have you ever seen the fairies? Do you know what they look like or where they might live?"

Wally nervously searched for an answer. He was taught not to lie, but he didn't want to tell her about the fairies he saw the day before. Wally's eyes darted around, and he rubbed his hands, "Well, I-I look for them sometimes and I *thought* I heard them in the woods once." He looked down.

Walinda sensed Wally was not telling her the whole truth and she pulled out her wand and pointed it directly at Wally's nose. "If you don't get me those fairies, Wally, you might find yourself in that pile of rocks."

Wally swallowed hard. His mouth was dry, and his hands began to sweat.

Walinda sent Wally back into the forest

# Fairy Berries

to gather rocks and search for the fairies. Hiking along the creek, the bag was heavier than ever. Wally carried it as long as he could. When it was too heavy to carry any further, he resorted to dragging it.

Wally needed a break. He sat near a tree with his eyes closed to catch his breath. He was almost asleep when he heard a squeaky sound. He perked up and listened closely. He followed the sound all the way to the edge of the creek. The water sparkled like diamonds, and Wally was captivated by it. What seemed like a mosquito flew by his ear and he swatted at it and missed. It flew by his nose. He swatted and missed again. Then the little "mosquito" landed right on the top of the weasel's head, and this time, he slapped at his head so hard that he fell backward into the creek!

Wally's arms and legs flailed about in the water. He coughed and spattered as he crawled out of the creek soaking wet. He was now determined to find whatever it was that landed on him.

He heard the sound again coming from down near the ground. He kneeled, pressing his

# Fairy Berries

ear toward the earth. Out of nowhere, a slew of acorns rained down on his head, followed by a squeaky little laugh.

Purple wings and hair hovered in front of Wally. He said, "You're a fairy! I thought you were supposed to be nice."

Lilly covered her heart with her hand and said, "I *am* nice! It's just that fairies love playing jokes. I didn't mean to make you angry with my teasing. I'm sorry. My name is Lilly. Can we be friends?"

Wally wasn't sure if he could trust the fairy. He stood with his head down, kicking at the grass with his foot.

The fairy giggled, flew around his neck, and tickled him with her flapping wings. That got a smile out of Wally. A warmth covered his heart and he felt less afraid. He said, "I'd like to be friends. I'm sorry I got angry."

Lilly fluttered her wings and said, "That's okay; I'm glad we're buddies now. Hey, I bet I can beat you to the top of that tree over there," as she pointed to one of the tallest trees in the forest.

# Fairy Berries

"Do you want to race?"

Wally looked over at Lilly, who was already flying up the tree! He quickly grabbed his bag and started running. He struggled and could barely move up the trunk of the tree. He finally made it to the top, gasping for air. "Hey, no fair! You started before I did!"

Lilly was there, pretending to sleep, but then she giggled and said, "I know. This didn't count, but it was fun, right? Wait, you would be much faster if you weren't carrying that huge bag, and why are you carrying it anyway? What's in it?"

Wally was standing on a tree branch, and the branch cracked as he tried to think of an answer.

# Fairy Berries

It cracked again, and before Wally could drag the bag and himself off the branch, it broke. Down he went, hitting every tree branch all the way to the forest floor, still clutching the bag. Acting quickly, Lilly used her fairy magic to slow him down. He landed softly on his feet and the only wounds he got were some light scratches from hitting the branches. Even so, Wally started shaking and crying.

Lilly flew down to him. "Oh, Wally, are you ok?" She gave him hugs.

Wally sniffed and said, "Yeah, I'm ok." He sat down and leaned on the bag. A few more tears fell.

Lilly looked at his scratches and flew over each one, putting a little fairy dust on them, to heal the scratches.

Wally said, "You saved my life!" He wiped his eyes and leaned forward, and they hugged.

Lilly sat down on Wally's bag, and the two friends sat quietly, thinking about what just happened.

Lilly asked again, "Wally, what's in this bag?

# Fairy Berries

It's hard, and it seems awfully heavy, and maybe that's why the branch broke. Do you carry it everywhere you go?"

"I need this bag! The witch … I mean, I just need it." Changing the subject, Wally said, "Let's go play some more. I'll leave the bag at the foot of the tree this time, but I will need to keep an eye on it, ok?"

Lilly agreed. "That sounds fine to me! Now, come on and let's race!"

CHAPTER SEVEN

# The Berries

Wally carefully put the bag down beside the tree, making sure he wouldn't get too far away from it. They raced up and down the tree playing tag, and he was amazed at how fast he could run.

Wally needed a rest after a while. He sat beside his bag, and Lilly wasn't far behind. She flipped in the air five times. *Do fairies ever get tired?*

Wally tapped on the bag and squirmed as he thought about telling Lilly about the witch. Instead of telling her that, he said, "I was in the forest one day, and I saw you and your fairy friends playing. I heard you singing a song about the fairy berries. Do you know the song I'm talking about?"

# Fairy Berries

Lilly clapped her hands, "Those fairies are my sisters." She flew in circles and began to sing, "A fairy you may meet, A berry you may eat, and when you do, you won't feel blue, you'll be so sweet!" She stopped an inch in front of Wally's nose, her face all a glow. "That one?"

"Yes, that's the one!" Wally said smiling. "Does that mean that the berries have special powers? Are the berries real?"

Lilly's eyes sparkled. "Yes, they're real, and they fill everyone who eats them with happiness and love." When she said "love" she did a backflip.

"Love?" Wally asked. "If someone eats a berry, their heart is immediately filled with happiness and love?"

Lilly rested on the bag. "I knew the meanest Troll ever, and he became like a sweet teddy bear after he ate a fairy berry." Lilly crossed her legs and inspected her fingernails.

"Wow! Where are these berries?" Wally asked.

The fairy said, "Oh, Wally, you silly weasel, they're in a berry patch!" And Lilly giggled so hard that she fell off the bag backwards.

# Fairy Berries

Lilly climbed back up on the bag, and Wally confessed, "I have some fairy dust." He slowly pulled some from his pocket.

"Where did you find the fairy dust?" Lilly asked.

"I found it where you and your sisters were playing. I kept it hoping it would help me find my parents."

"Where did your parents go?" Lilly asked.

"I don't know. One day I was in the forest playing with my friends and looking for … fairies … and I came home, and my parents were gone. I haven't seen them since that day." Lilly listened and put her hand on his. This encouraged Wally to tell her more, "Walinda the witch found me, and I have to live with her now." Wally looked at Lilly sheepishly.

Lilly saw how sad and scared Wally was. "I have a surprise for you Wally." She brought out from behind her back the fattest purple berry he'd ever seen. "A fairy berry, special for you."

His eyes almost burst out of his head. This special berry just for him? He believed it would

# Fairy Berries

fill him with love so without waiting, he popped the berry right into his mouth and its sugary juices exploded. He savored the sweetness and swallowed; his cheeks grew warm, and his eyes were watery as he remembered his mother and father and how much they loved him. He felt free from Walinda, even though he wasn't yet. Love, for himself and everyone, surged through his heart and his entire body. He felt strong and brave.

Wally hadn't felt this joyful in a long time. He loved Lilly and appreciated everything she did

for him that day.

He started thinking about Walinda and couldn't help but wonder what would happen if she ate a berry. Could it turn such a wretched witch into a nice loving one?

Wally listened while Lilly told him that Walinda planned to destroy the fairies and their berries.

"Aren't you afraid?" Wally asked. He remembered how scared he felt when Walinda chanted over the big black pot.

"Afraid of that old witch? No way!" Lilly said.

"Why not? She's mean and powerful," Wally replied.

Lilly leaned back and said, "Because the power of love is stronger than her kind of power. Love always wins."

Wally leaned back, too, and closed his eyes. Lilly was about to tell him what Walinda had been doing to the forest and the animals, but then … WHAM!

CHAPTER EIGHT

# Walinda's War

Wally covered his head and cried out. When he opened his eyes, Walinda was standing over him, her wand pointed at his face.

"What have you been doing all this time?! Sleeping?! I've been waiting for hours for you to come back with information about the fairies and I've heard nothing from you!"

Wally rubbed his forehead. "I-I-I thought I heard some fairies and was listening hard to find out where the sounds were coming from so that I could take you to them."

"It looked like you were taking a nap to me," Walinda snorted.

Walinda backed off and put her wand away. "Get up! Let's go find those fairies!"

Wally was relieved that Walinda didn't see

# Fairy Berries

Lilly. He also wondered if Lilly had heard what he said to Walinda. He worried that his words had hurt her feelings and she wouldn't want to be his friend anymore. He looked around for her and listened for her giggle and the flutter of her wings, but he heard nothing. She was gone.

Walinda and Wally searched for a long time. Wally carried the bag of rocks on his back, hunched over from its heavy weight, but he kept his eyes open wide for his parents and for Lilly.

Walinda walked behind Wally. "Wally, if we don't find those fairies soon, I'm turning you into a stone. You're no good to me anymore if you can't find the fairies!" She poked him with her wand as they hunted.

They had almost reached Wally's old house when he heard giggling, lots of giggling. The witch heard it too.

"Shshsh! Stop! It's the fairies! Get out of my way, Wally. Those little winged creatures have no hope now!" She pushed Wally aside and pointed her wand in the direction of the giggles.

The giggling ended suddenly, and the forest

# Fairy Berries

was perfectly quiet. Walinda stared intently, searching the trees with her beady green eyes. In a chorus, the fairies sang.

*A fairy you may meet.*
*A berry you may eat.*
*And when you do,*
*you won't feel blue.*
*You'll be so sweet!*

Green steam came out of Walinda's ears. She flung her wand's power everywhere. The fairies flew about, zigging and zagging, to get out of harm's way.

Hiding high up in the trees, the fairies launched berries at Walinda, trying to get one in her mouth. They knew that eating even one fairy berry could turn her into a nice witch.

Wally shivered behind a rock. He poked his head out and couldn't believe what he saw. Almost every tree was gray, the flowers and grass were brown, and every living animal that got in the path of Walinda's wand turned to stone.

# Fairy Berries

As she unleashed all her rage into the forest, Walinda clenched her lips so that no berries could land in her mouth. Wally knew he had to come up with a plan before she destroyed the entire forest and hurt Lilly and the other fairies. It was risky, but Wally knew he had no other choice.

# Fairy Berries

He grabbed the bag full of stones and slowly crawled out from behind the rock, trying to stay hidden from the witch. Sparks were flying near his head and bouncing off trees with a loud cracking sound. His arm ached as he pulled the bag across the dirt, inching closer to the witch.

Walinda stood on a rock pointing her wand, casting its destructive power at the fairies.

Groaning and with sweat pouring down his face, Wally heaved himself up onto the rock and lifted the bag high above his head.

Walinda sneered at his shaking arms and legs and pointed her wand between Wally's eyebrows. "I should have done this a long time ago," she growled.

With every ounce of strength, he yelled back, "You can't hurt me or the fairies any more!" and slammed the bag down onto the witch's foot.

The witch stood frozen like a statue. But then her mouth opened wide and she let out the loudest scream, a screech. *EEEEOOOOWWW!* Everyone covered their ears.

The four fairy sisters saw their chance

## Fairy Berries

and launched four berries at the same time—1, 2, 3, 4—and they landed right in Walinda's mouth!

The witch couldn't help but bite down on the berries. She jumped up and down holding her foot saying "ow, ow, ow," as she swallowed the sweet berries.

Walinda dropped her wand. She wibbled and she wobbled. Everyone thought she might fall over. With one hand on her heart and the other on her cheek, she said, "Those berries are the most delicious things I've ever tasted in my entire life!"

A look of concern came over her face, though, as a low rumbling churned in her tummy. All the meanness gathered up inside her and bubbled up like a volcano. Was she going to explode? Her face was red. Her eyes were as big as cookies. Her head swayed back and forth. Then the witch let out the longest, loudest burp. With her hand over her mouth, she giggled and said, "Oh, my, excuse me."

The darkness in Walinda's green eyes left, changing them to bright blue. She looked around the forest and asked, mostly to herself, "What have I done?" She gazed at the gray trees, the brown grass, and broken flowers. She could see that she had done something terrible to the fairies and to the forest and all the wonderful living plants and animals. "I'm so sorry for what I've done here today! For what I've been doing every day. I've been so … wicked! Can you forgive me?!"

Walinda picked up her wand. A stream of blue magical power, like living water, flowed from her wand to the branches of the trees. The forest changed back to its healthy greens, blues, yellows, and reds. It was beginning to look and sound like the beautiful place it once was, and the birds began to sing.

Just then, Lilly shrieked, "Wally!"

In all the chaos, no one had noticed Wally. He lay at the bottom of the rock Walinda stood upon. He had been turned to stone.

The fairies flew over to Wally and put fairy dust on him. But Walinda had created a spell that only she could reverse.

## Fairy Berries

Walinda reached down and picked up the stone. Holding it gently in her hands, she said,

"Mean and cruelty was my art,
But eating berries changed my heart.
I pledge today to change my ways.
Take them back to their earlier days!"

Mist surrounded Walinda, spinning around her like a storm. The fairies backed away as Walinda and the stone disappeared into the dark cloud.

## Fairy Berries

The bag of rocks stirred and began to shake, vibrating the ground. Each stone rose up out of the bag. They floated above the ground and swirled together in rhythm, like planets in their own universe. Slowly at first, then faster and faster until a puff of smoke covered them. As the smoke cleared, there were no more rocks. Instead eight rabbits, three squirrels, a raccoon, and two weasels appeared! And one Wally. Everyone shrieked with joy.

The spell was broken. Wally was alive again!

Two weasels ran toward Wally with their arms stretched out for an embrace. Wally exclaimed, "Mom!? Dad!? Is that you?" He could barely see through the tears pooling in his eyes.

"Yes, honey, it's us. We're back together again! We love you, son!" And the three of them hugged. Wally said, "I've missed you so much!"

Walinda wiped a tear away and said, "Wally, I'm so sorry for what I did to you and your parents." She added, "I've got a lot of work to do, finding all the little animals I turned into rocks. I promise to change them all back into the furry friends they once were."

Wally turned to Lilly. "I'm sorry about bringing the witch near you and your berries and the fairy village. I hope you can forgive me."

Lilly flew by his neck, tickling him and said, "Wally, there's nothing to forgive. We are favorite friends. I hid when Walinda hit you in the head, and I heard her say that she would hurt you if you didn't find the berries. I flew back to the fairy village and told the other fairies everything. Faye and Jada were in charge of getting the fairies to gather as many berries as they could, and Felicia found where you were so that we could hide in the trees. Our plan was to protect you."

Wally's heart leapt; he kicked at the grass a little and said, "You're my favorite friend, too, Lilly! You made my wish come true—I have my parents back."

"Wally, you were so brave today. It was the love within you that gave you the courage to fight Walinda. And maybe a little magic from us," she said with a wink.

Mr. and Mrs. Weasel, Wally, Lilly and all the

## Fairy Berries

fairies spent the rest of the day talking and eating and playing in the woods. Alice, Taylor, and Andy also joined them for the fun.

The Weasel family made a new home for themselves right outside of the fairy village and every day, Lilly and Wally played high up in the trees until the sun set.

## THE END

# About the Author

Allison Stevens is the author of *Fairy Berries*. She loves to help children know that they can change their world through imagination. A fanatic dog lover, she provides dog-sitting for rescues and volunteers at her local humane society. Movies, music, and books trigger her imagination so she can tell beautiful and adventurous stories. Allison stays busy with her two grandchildren and husband in Grand Rapids, Michigan.

## Connect with the Author

allisonleighstevens.com

## Leave a Review

If you enjoyed this book, will you please consider writing a review on your platform of choice? Reviews help self-published authors make their books more visible to new readers.

Made in the USA
Las Vegas, NV
15 March 2024